The Dun Horse

and other horse stories

Compiled by Vic Parker

Miles
Kelly

First published in 2014 by Miles Kelly Publishing Ltd
Harding's Barn, Bardfield End Green, Thaxted, Essex, CM6 3PX, UK

2 4 6 8 10 9 7 5 3 1

Publishing Director Belinda Gallagher
Creative Director Jo Cowan
Editorial Director Rosie Neave
Senior Editor Claire Philip
Designer Rob Hale
Production Manager Elizabeth Collins
Reprographics Stephan Davis, Jennifer Hunt, Thom Allaway

ISBN 978-1-78209-652-8

Printed in China

British Library Cataloguing-in-Publication Data
A catalogue record for this book is available from the British Library

ACKNOWLEDGEMENTS
The publishers would like to thank the following artists who have contributed to this book:
Advocate Art: Simon Mendez (Cover)
Beehive Illustration: Iole Rosa, Gail Yerrill
The Bright Agency: Mélanie Florian, Kirsteen Harris-Jones (borders)

Made with paper from a sustainable forest

www.mileskelly.net
info@mileskelly.net

Contents

Sigurd the Hero and his Good Horse Grani

By Andrew Lang

Sigurd and his horse, Grani, are heroes of Norse mythology – the ancient stories of the Vikings. Their tale was passed down for generations by storytellers who told it aloud, before it was written down in an Icelandic book called the Volsunga Saga, *over 700 years ago.*

ONCE UPON A TIME there was a king in the north who had won many wars. He was very old, but he took a beautiful young princess to be his new wife.

However, in the midst of his happiness, a

jealous king who had wanted to marry the princess himself came up against him with a great army.

The old king went out and fought bravely, but eventually his sword broke and he was gravely wounded. Sad to say, all his men fled, leaving him for dead.

But in the night, when the battle was over, his young wife came out and searched for him among the slain. At last she found him and asked whether he might be healed. But he said no, his luck was gone, his sword was broken, and he must die. He then told her that she would have a son, and that son would be a great warrior, and he would avenge his death. He bade her keep the broken pieces of the sword, to make a new sword for his son, and that blade should be called Gram. Then he died.

The wife's maid then came up to her and said, "In case the enemy finds us, we must change clothes – you pretend to be me and I will pretend to be you."

So they swapped clothes, and hid together in a nearby wood. It wasn't long, however, before they were discovered and captured by strangers, who carried them away in a ship to Denmark.

There, when they were brought before the king, he thought the maid looked like a queen, and the queen like a maid. So he asked the queen, "How do you know in the dark of night whether morning is near?"

And she said, "I know because, when I

was younger, I used to have to rise and light the fires, and still I wake at the same time."

'A strange queen to light the fires,' thought the king.

Then he asked the queen, who was dressed like a maid, "How do you know in the dark of night whether morning is drawing near?"

"My father gave me a gold ring," said she, "and it always grows cold on my finger when dawn comes."

"It would be a very strange house if the maids wore gold!" said the king. "Truly you are no maid, but a king's daughter."

Fortunately he was a good man, who treated her as royalty should be.

As time went on the queen had a son,

who she called Sigurd. He was a beautiful boy and very strong. Sigurd had a tutor to look after him and teach him about all things. One day, the tutor told Sigurd to go to the king and ask for a horse.

"Go and choose one – you can have any one you like," said the king.

But Sigurd did not go to the royal stables, as might be expected. Instead, he went out into the wood where the wild horses grazed. There he met an old man with a white beard, and he said to him, "Come! Please help me choose a horse."

The old man told him to drive all the horses into the river. Only one swam across, and that was the one that Sigurd chose. Unbeknown to Sigurd, the old man was the

father of the gods, Odin, and the horse
Sigurd had chosen had been bred from
Odin's own horse, Sleipnir. Sigurd called
him Grani, and he proved to be the best
horse ever.

When Sigurd had grown to be a warrior,
he heard that somewhere to the south there
was a beautiful lady under a
spell. She had to sleep in

a castle, surrounded by a fire until a knight could rescue her. Sigurd decided to end the enchantment himself.

When they arrived at the castle, Sigurd and Grani headed fearlessly towards the fire, and leaped through it. They climbed up to the topmost tower and when Sigurd entered, he saw a figure dressed in armour – it was the beautiful lady sleeping. She awoke when he took off her helmet, and said, "Sigurd has broken the spell at last!"

So the curse was lifted. The beautiful lady and Sigurd loved each other and lived happily ever after.

The Dun Horse

Edited by Hamilton Wright Mabie

*This story is a Native American folktale. The Pawnee were
a farming people who lived around the Missouri River, in modern-
day Nebraska and northern Kansas in the United States.*

MANY YEARS AGO, there lived in the
Pawnee tribe an old woman and her
sixteen-year-old grandson. They had no
relations and were very poor – so poor that
they were looked down on by the rest of the
tribe. They had nothing of their own, so
always, after the village started to move the

camp from one place to another, these two would stay behind, to pick up anything that the other Indians had thrown away.

Now, it happened one day, after the tribe had moved away from the camp, that this old woman and her boy were following along the trail behind the rest, when they came to a miserable old dun horse.

The poor old thing was exhausted. He was blind in one eye, and had a bad back. In fact, he was so downtrodden that none of the Pawnees had been willing to take the trouble to try to drive him along with them. He had been left behind.

But when the old woman and her boy came along, the boy said, "Come now, we will take this poor old horse, and care for him – he can help us carry our pack."

So the old woman put her pack on the horse and drove him along, though he limped and could only go very slowly.

The tribe moved on until they came to Court House Rock. The two poor Indians followed them and camped with the others. One day soon after, the news spread that a large herd of buffalo were near and that among them was a spotted calf.

The Head Chief of the Pawnees had a very beautiful daughter, and when he heard about the spotted calf, he ordered his old crier to go through the village and call out that the man who killed the spotted calf should have his daughter for his wife. To have a spotted robe was a very grand thing indeed within the Pawnee tribe.

So all the warriors and the young men picked out their best and fastest horses, and made ready to charge upon the herd.

Among them was the poor boy on the old dun horse. But when they saw him, all the rich young braves on their fast horses pointed at him and laughed.

The Dun Horse

When they stopped, the horse turned his head round and said to the boy in a quiet voice, "Do not ride back to the warriors who laugh at you because you have a poor horse. Stay here until the word is given to charge." The boy was so surprised to hear a talking horse that he did as he was told.

Soon all the fine horses were drawn up in line and pranced about, and they were so eager to go that their riders could hardly hold them in. At last the old crier gave the word, "Loo-ah!" – Go!

The Pawnees all leaned forwards on their horses and yelled, and away they went. The old dun horse did not seem to run. Instead he seemed to sail along like a graceful bird. He passed all the fastest horses and in a moment was among the buffalo. The boy easily picked out the spotted calf and, charging up alongside of it, let loose an arrow, straight and true. The calf fell instantly. Then the boy drew another arrow, which took down a large cow.

The boy slid off the back of the old dun horse to the ground – but how changed the animal was! He pranced about and would hardly stand still. His back was all right again, his legs were well and fine, and both his eyes were clear and bright.

The boy skinned the calf and the cow, and made two robes, then he prepared all the meat carefully and packed it up for the horse to carry. The boy put the spotted robe on the very top, and started back to the

17

camp on foot leading the dun horse.

Now the other warriors got back to camp shortly before the boy. They went to the old woman and said to her, "Your grandson has killed the spotted calf."

The old woman didn't believe them, but soon the boy came along leading the young-looking, prancing dun horse. The boy said to her, "Here, I have brought you plenty of meat to eat, and here is a robe, that you may have for yourself." Then the old woman laughed, for her heart was glad.

That night the horse spoke again to the boy and said, "Tonight, leave me behind that big hill, and in the morning come for me." The boy did as he was told and in the morning, when he went for the horse, he found with him a beautiful white gelding.

That night the dun horse told the boy to do the same, and when the boy went for him again, he found with him a beautiful black gelding. And so for ten nights, he left the horse among the hills, and each morning he found a different coloured horse – and all of them finer than any horses that the Pawnees had ever had in their tribe before.

When the boy grew up he married the daughter of the Head Chief, and lived happily in the village with his grandmother, the dun horse and his herd of horses.

Going for the Doctor

From *Black Beauty* by Anna Sewell

In this extract from Black Beauty *the young horse lives on the country estate of a wealthy landowner called Squire Gordon, whose wife is dangerously ill. Here, Black Beauty saves the day despite being placed in grave danger.*

ONE NIGHT, I had eaten my hay and was lying down in my straw fast asleep, when I was suddenly roused by the stable bell ringing very loudly. I heard the door of the coachman's house open and the feet of my groom, John, running up the drive to the squire's hall.

He was back again in no time – he unlocked the stable door and came in, calling out, "Wake up, Beauty! You must go fast now, if ever you did."

Almost before I could think, he had got the saddle on my back and the bridle on my head, and he then took me at a quick trot up to the hall door.

Squire Gordon stood there, with a lamp in his hand. "Now, John," he said, "ride for your life – that is, for your mistress's life, there is not a moment to lose. Give this note to Dr White, then give your horse a rest at the inn and be back as soon as you can."

John said, "Yes, sir," and was on my back in a minute.

Then we were off through
the park, and through the
village, and down the hill
till we came to
a long piece
of level road by
the riverside.

John said to me,
"Now, Beauty, do your
best." And so I did. For two
miles I galloped as fast as I
could, I don't believe that my old
grandfather, who was a prize-winning
racehorse, could have gone faster.

When we came to the bridge John pulled
me up a little and patted my neck. "Well
done, Beauty! Good old fellow," he said.

He would have let me go slower, but my spirit was up, and I was off again, galloping as fast as before.

After eight miles' run we came to the town, through the streets and into the market place. It was all quite still except the clatter of my feet on the stones – everybody was asleep. The church clock struck three as we drew up at Dr White's door. John rang the bell twice and then knocked at the door like thunder. A window was thrown up and Dr White, in his nightcap, put his head out and said, "What do you want?"

"Mrs Gordon is very ill, sir. Master wants you to come at once – he thinks she will die if you cannot get there. Here is a note."

"Wait," he said, "I will come."

He shut the window and was soon at the door to speak to John.

"The worst of it is," he said, "that my horse has been out all day and is quite exhausted, my son has my other one and he is away. What is to be done? Can I have your horse?"

"He has come at a gallop nearly all the way, sir, and I was to give him a rest here – but I think my master would not be against it, if you think fit, sir."

"All right," the doctor said, "I will soon be ready to go."

John stood by me and stroked my neck. I was very hot. The doctor came out with his riding-whip.

"You need not take that, sir," said John,

"Black Beauty will go till he drops. Take care of him, sir, if you can. I should not like any harm to come to him."

"Of course, John," said the doctor, and in a minute we had left John far behind.

I will not tell about our way back. The doctor was a heavier man than John and not so good a rider, however, I did my very best. By the time we reached the park, I was very nearly spent. The groom's boy, Joe, was at the lodge gate and my master was at the hall door, waiting. My master spoke not a word as the doctor went into the house with him. Then Joe led me to the stable.

I was glad to get home – my legs shook under me and I could only stand and pant. I had not a dry hair on my body, the sweat ran down my legs and I steamed all over. Joe was young and small, but he did the very best for me that he knew. He rubbed my legs and chest, but he did not put my warm cloth on me – he thought I was so hot I should not like it.

Then he gave me a pailful of water to drink. It was cold and very good, and I drank it all. Then he gave me some hay and some corn and, thinking he had done right, he went away.

Soon I began to shake and tremble and turned deadly cold. My legs ached, my loins ached, and my chest ached, and I felt sore all over. Oh, how I wished for my warm thick cloth, as I stood and trembled! I wished for John, but he had eight miles to

walk, so I lay down in my straw and
tried to go to sleep.

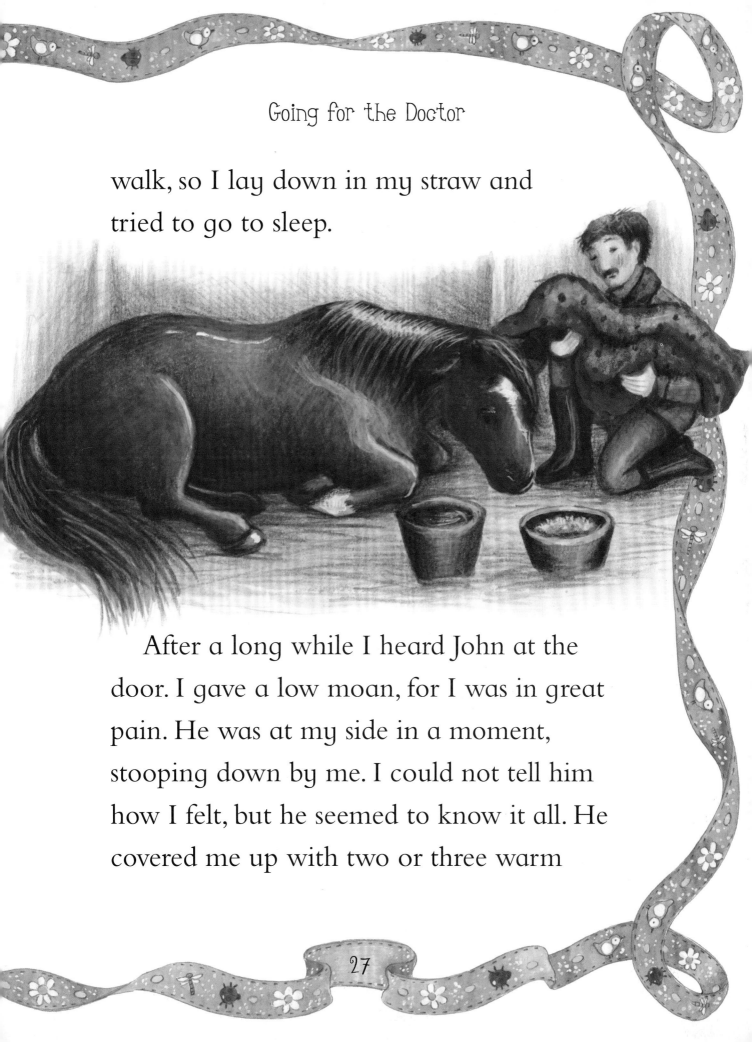

After a long while I heard John at the
door. I gave a low moan, for I was in great
pain. He was at my side in a moment,
stooping down by me. I could not tell him
how I felt, but he seemed to know it all. He
covered me up with two or three warm

cloths and then ran to the house for some hot water. He made me some warm gruel, which I drank, and then I fell fast asleep.

The next day, I became very ill. A strong inflammation attacked my lungs, and I could not draw my breath without pain. John nursed me round the clock – he would get up two or three times in the night to come to me. My master, too, often came to see me, until I was better.

"My poor Beauty," he said one day, "my good horse, you saved your mistress's life, Beauty. Yes, you saved her life." I was very glad to hear that.

Apparently, the doctor had said that if we had been a little longer it would have been too late. John told my master he never

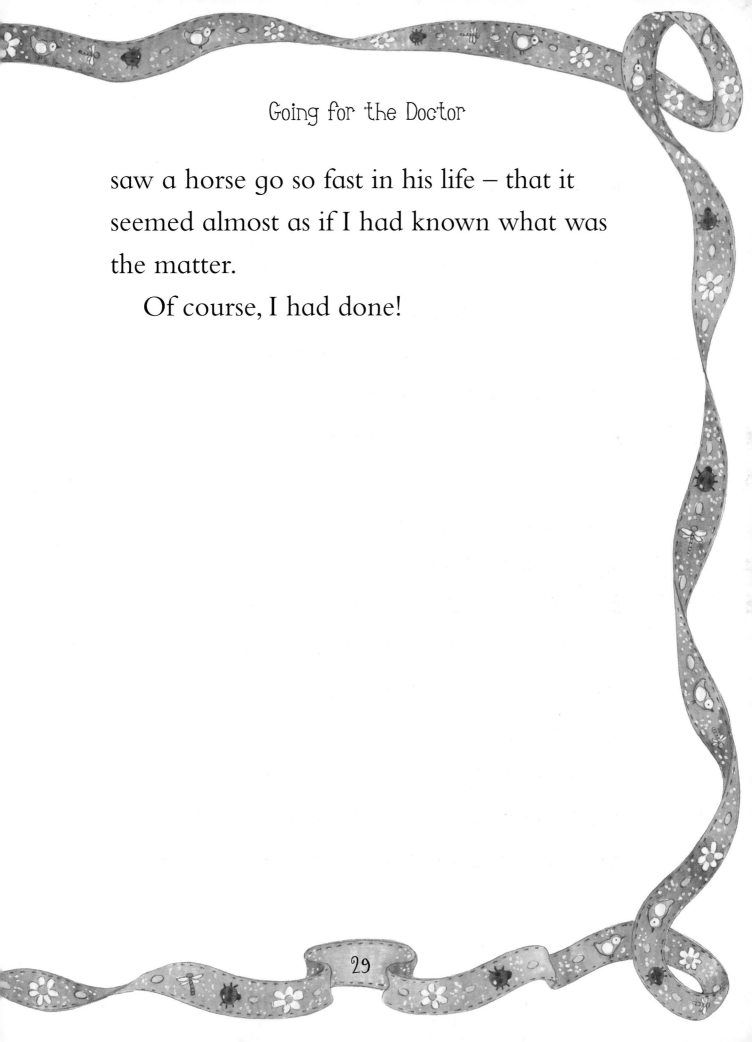

saw a horse go so fast in his life – that it seemed almost as if I had known what was the matter.

Of course, I had done!

Taming the Colt

From *Little Men* by Louisa M Alcott

Jo Bhaer and her husband run Plumfield School for mischievous boys. They encourage the students to develop an interest to help them become responsible young people. In this extract, a fourteen-year-old orphan called Dan finds an exciting pursuit…

A FINE YOUNG HORSE of Mr Laurie's was kept at Plumfield that summer, running loose in a large pasture across the brook. The boys were all interested in the handsome, spirited creature, affectionately known as Prince Charlie. For a time they were fond of watching him gallop and frisk with his plumey tail flying and his handsome head in the air. But they soon got tired of it and left the horse to himself. All but Dan – he never tired of looking at Charlie, and seldom failed to visit him each day with a lump of sugar, a bit of bread or an apple to make him feel welcome.

Charlie was grateful, accepted his friendship, and the two loved one another. In whatever part of the wide field he might be, Charlie always came at full speed when Dan whistled at the fence bars, and the boy was never happier than when the beautiful creature put its head on his shoulder, looking up at him with fine eyes full of intelligent affection.

"We understand one another, don't we, old fellow?" Dan would say, proud of the horse's confidence. He was so protective of their friendship that he never asked anyone to accompany him on these daily visits.

Mr Laurie came now and then to see how Charlie got on. One day, he spoke of having him broken-in in the autumn.

"He won't need much taming, he is so gentle and fine-tempered. I shall come out and try him with a saddle myself some day," Mr Laurie said.

"He lets me put a halter on him, but I don't believe he will bear a saddle even if you put it on," answered Dan.

"I shall coax him to bear it and I won't mind a few tumbles at first. He has never

been harshly treated, so I don't think he will be too frightened."

"I wonder what he would do," said Dan to himself, as Mr Laurie went away.

A daring fancy to try the experiment took possession of the boy as he sat on the topmost rail with the glossy back temptingly near him.

Never thinking of danger, Dan quickly and quietly took his seat. He did not keep it long, however, for with an astonished snort, Charlie reared straight up and threw Dan onto the ground. The fall did not hurt him – the turf was soft and he jumped up, saying, with a laugh, "I did it anyway! Come here, you rascal, and I'll try it again."

But Charlie refused to approach and Dan left him with his mind made up to get him in the end.

Next time, Dan took a halter and after putting it on the horse, played with Charlie for a while, leading him to and fro, and putting him through various antics till he was a little tired. Then Dan sat on the wall and gave Charlie some bread, waiting for a good chance to grab the halter and slip onto his back. Charlie tried the old trick, but Dan held on. Charlie was amazed and, after prancing for a minute, set off at a gallop – away went Dan, heels over head, and he landed on the ground. He lay still, collecting his wits, while Charlie tore round the field, tossing his head with satisfaction.

Presently it seemed to occur to the horse that something was wrong with Dan and he went to see what the matter was. Dan let him sniff about, then looked up at him, saying, "You think you have won, but you are mistaken, old boy, and I'll ride you yet – just see if I don't."

Dan tried no more that day, but soon after attempted a new method. He strapped a folded blanket on Charlie's back and then let him race, and rear, and roll, and fume as much as he liked.

After a few times Charlie calmed down

and, in a few days, he permitted Dan to mount him. Dan patted and praised him, and took a short turn every day. He fell off frequently, but kept trying again in spite of that. He longed to try a saddle and bridle, but dared not tell anyone what he had done. However, unbeknown to him, the school caretaker, Silas, had seen him and put in a good word for him.

"Dan has been breaking the colt in, sir," Silas told Mr Bhaer one night, chuckling.

"How do you know?" asked the astonished school master.

"Well, when Dan kept going off to the pasture and coming home black and blue, I thought that something must be going on. So I crept up to the field and spied on him,

and I saw him going through all manner of games with Charlie. He was thrown about and knocked around like a sack of grain, but the plucky boy kept on going."

"But, Silas, you should have stopped it – the boy might have been killed," said Mr Bhaer, wondering what on earth the pupils might get up to next.

"The fact was, he was doing so well I couldn't bring myself to stop it," replied Silas. "But now I know he's hankerin' after a saddle, so I thought I'd tell you and maybe you'd let him try. Mr Laurie won't mind, and Charlie's all the better for it."

"We shall see," and off went Mr Bhaer to inquire into the matter.

Dan owned up at once, and was eager to show everyone how well he could ride the horse. He proudly proved that Silas was right by showing off his power over Charlie, for by much coaxing, many carrots and infinite staying power, he really had succeeded in riding the colt with a halter and blanket. Mr Laurie was very much

amused and well pleased with Dan's
courage, determination and skill.

He set about Charlie's education at once
and, thanks to Dan, the horse took kindly
to the saddle and bridle. After Mr Laurie
had trained him a little, Dan was permitted
to ride him.

"Isn't he handsome?" said Dan one day
as he dismounted and stood with his arm
round Charlie's neck.

"Yes, and isn't he a much more
agreeable animal than the wild colt who
spent his days racing about the field and
running away now and then?" asked
Mrs Bhaer from the steps where she
was watching.

"Of course he is. See he won't run away

now, even if I don't hold him. I have tamed him well, haven't I?"

Dan looked both proud and pleased – as well he might, for, in spite of their struggles together, Charlie loved him even better than his master.

"I am taming a colt too, and I think I shall succeed as well as you if I am as patient and persevering," said Mrs Jo, smiling significantly at Dan.

And Dan understood she meant him!

"We won't jump over the fence and run away. We will stay and let them make a handsome, useful young man of us, hey, Charlie?" he said, laughing, yet in earnest.